David Copperfield

Charles Dickens

TEACHER GUIDE

NOTE:

The trade book edition of the novel used to prepare this guide is found in the Novel Units catalog and on the Novel Units website. Using other editions may have varied page references.

Please note: We have assigned Interest Levels based on our knowledge of the themes and ideas of the books included in the Novel Units sets, however, please assess the appropriateness of this novel or trade book for the age level and maturity of your students prior to reading with them. You know your students best!

ISBN 978-1-56137-510-3

To order, contact your local school supply store, or:

Toll-Free Fax: 877.716.7272
Phone: 888.650.4224
3901 Union Blvd., Suite 155
St. Louis, MO 63115

sales@novelunits.com

novelunits.com

Table of Contents

Introduction

"But, like many fond parents, I have in my heart of hearts a favorite child. And his name is David Copperfield." —Charles Dickens

David Copperfield was written when Dickens was in his mid-thirties, at a time when his popularity with his countrymen was already well-established. It was issued in serial form from May 1849, through November 1850, in twenty installments, each one awaited with greater anticipation than the last by a thoroughly enchanted public. The novel has delighted countless readers since. It is one of the "must-reads" of English literature.

Dickens' talent for creating realistic, enduring characters has been compared to Shakespeare's, as have his stylistic genius, his wit, and his prolificacy. The characters in *David Copperfield* seem ready to walk off the pages, and even after the final page has been turned, the self-serving Murdstones, unearthly Uriah Heep, the eloquent and usually penniless Mr. Micawber, innocent Little Em'ly, practical but kindly Aunt Betsey, hopelessly childish Dora, and the angelic Agnes Wickfield live on in the reader's memory.

David Copperfield is written in the first-person, a long retrospective that is autobiographical in many respects. Noting the differences and similarities in how the plot of the novel compares to the events of Dickens' own life is an interesting activity for students. While David's problems began when his widowed mother married the villainous Murdstone and then died, Dickens' problems were the result of his living father's improvidence. Both Dickens and David spent grim and frightening periods as child laborers—David in a wine merchants' warehouse and Dickens in a shoeblacking factory. Dickens' romantic attraction to Maria Beadnell was ended by her parents, who felt he was beneath their daughter. David's similar attraction to Dora was almost squashed by her father—but he conveniently died, leaving his daughter, with limited assets, in the care of two maiden aunts who doted on David and happily gave their permission for the marriage. Like Dickens, David worked in an attorney's office after completing school, then became a newspaper reporter and later a novelist. It seems that Mr. Micawber was based on Dickens' father, and that Dora's difficulties with housekeeping were modeled on similar problems Dickens experienced in his marriage to Catherine Hogarth.

In the course of the novel, David experiences feelings in his "undisciplined heart" that are universally human—fear, loneliness, grief, joy, friendship, romantic love. His candor about these feelings endears him to us. By the end of the novel, David has matured through his various experiences with his own goodness and decency intact, finally deserving of the angelic Agnes. In true Dickensian style, David's triumph is one of the individual over the system—of generosity and warmth of spirit over greed and dishonesty.

Summary

The night David Copperfield was born at Blunderstone, Suffolk, his great-aunt, Miss Betsey Trotwood, left the house abruptly because she had been hoping for a girl who would bear her name. David's father had died six months before he was born. David's young mother, Clara, and devoted nurse, Peggotty, cared for him tenderly.

Mr. Murdstone courted David's mother, and after they married, Murdstone proved to be stingy and cruel. To make matters worse, Mr. Murdstone's sister, Jane, came to take charge of the household. The one bright spot in David's unhappy childhood was a trip with Peggotty to Yarmouth, where her brother lived with two adopted children, Little Em'ly and Ham, in a boat that had been converted into a little house.

After an altercation with Murdstone, David was sent off to Salem House, a miserable school near London overseen by a consummately unfair and unfeeling headmaster, Creakle. David's stay at Salem House was tolerable only because of his friendships with Tommy Traddles and James Steerforth.

When David's mother and her infant died, Murdstone put David to work in the warehouse of Murdstone and Grinby, Wine Merchants. With too much work to do, and never enough to eat, 10-year-old David was grateful for the kindnesses of his landlord, Wilkins Micawber. But Micawber, haunted by creditors, moved to Plymouth and David decided to run away to Betsey Trotwood's home in Dover.

He was soon robbed of all his possessions and money, but struggled to Dover anyway. Miss Betsey, still a bit angry at David for not being a girl, sought the advice of her lodger, the simple-minded Mr. Dick, who suggested they begin by giving David a bath. Miss Betsey wrote to Murdstone to claim his stepson, but upon meeting the Murdstones and realizing how detestable they were, she refused to let David leave.

Aunt Betsey sent David to a school in Canterbury, where he boarded with Aunt Betsey's lawyer, Mr. Wickfield, and his daughter, Agnes, who quickly became David's dear friend. Also at the Wickfield's was Uriah Heep, Wickfield's clerk, whose strange appearance and obsequious manner disgusted David. School at Canterbury was much different than at Salem House, and David developed a great respect for the headmaster, Dr. Strong.

After graduating at 17, David took some time to decide on a profession. He renewed acquaintance with Steerforth, visiting his home and meeting his mother and a girl named Rosa Dartle, who was obviously in love with Steerforth. Afterwards, Steerforth and David went to Yarmouth. In spite of Em'ly's engagement to Ham, she and Steerforth were instantly attracted to one another, although David didn't seem to notice.

When David saw Agnes Wickfield, she warned him that Steerforth should not be trusted, and confessed that she feared Uriah Heep was taking over her father's business as he began to show signs of senility. Later on, David encountered Uriah, who offered the information that someday he hoped to marry Agnes.

When David decided he wanted to be a lawyer, he was articled to the firm of Spenlow and Jorkins. When he was invited to the Spenlow home and met Dora, his employer's daughter, he fell completely in love. The attraction was mutual, and they became secretly engaged.

David's happiness over his relationship with Dora was marred by the news of several crises: Steerforth and Little Em'ly had run away together, David's Aunt Betsey had lost all her money, and Uriah Heep had become Mr. Wickfield's partner.

Aunt Betsey moved in with David, with Mr. Dick renting a room close by, and David took a part-time job as Dr. Strong's secretary to help out with tight finances. Mr. Dick helped out, too, as a copy clerk for Tommy Traddles, now a lawyer. David also studied shorthand so he could become a parliamentary reporter.

When Miss Murdstone, employed as a companion to Dora, found David's love letters to the young lady, she promptly showed them to Mr. Spenlow. Spenlow accused David of going after Dora for the money she would inherit, and told him he forbade the match. On Spenlow's subsequent sudden death, it was learned that he had lived beyond his means and that Dora was almost penniless.

At 21, David and Dora married, but David's hope that marriage would cause Dora to grow up proved fruitless. After numerous attempts to improve Dora's housekeeping, and the loss of their baby, David decided to accept Dora exactly as she was. After the miscarriage, Dora's health began to decline steadily, though her spirits remained as high as ever. During this time, David published his first novel.

Mr. Micawber had crossed David's path several times by now, and David was surprised to learn that Micawber was now employed as Uriah Heep's clerk. Micawber, who had always been honest and full of warmth and friendship in the past, had now become mysteriously unlike himself.

The mystery was soon solved—Micawber revealed to Agnes, Aunt Betsey, David, and Traddles that Heep had been cheating Mr. Wickfield for years, and that Aunt Betsey's financial losses were also his fault. On exposure, Heep soon made restitution, and Mr. Wickfield even seemed more like he had years before.

Meanwhile, David had learned that Steerforth had deserted Little Em'ly somewhere in Europe. Mr. Peggotty had been traveling all over trying to find her, and with the help of Martha, a "fallen woman" to whom Em'ly had once been kind, she was found. Mr. Peggotty decided to take Em'ly to Australia, where they could make a new start. The Micawbers accompany them, thanks to a "loan" from Aunt Betsey.

Dora's health continued to fail, and David grew despondent. With Agnes' help, David somehow got through the last stages of Dora's illness. It was Agnes who told him that she was gone, and Agnes who suggested that David go abroad to recover from the trauma.

He went to Yarmouth first to deliver a letter from Em'ly to Ham, but a terrible storm came up, and Ham made a valiant but unsuccessful attempt to rescue a seaman clinging to a ship in distress off the coast. The seaman Ham died trying to save was Steerforth.

After three years in Europe, David realized the importance of Agnes' friendship—and discovered he wanted her to be his wife. This had been Agnes' fondest secret wish since childhood, and they soon married.

The novel ends with a present-tense chapter: Micawber is a magistrate in Australia, and Emily and Mr. Peggotty are happy. Aunt Betsey, Peggotty, and Mr. Dick live near David and his growing family, and David's career as a novelist is well underway.

About the Author

Charles Dickens was born in Landport, Portsea, England, on February 7, 1812, the second of eight children. A precocious child, he learned to read at an early age and eagerly devoured stories by Fielding, Defoe, Goldsmith, and others. His father, a clerk at the Navy Pay Office, had trouble supporting his large family and was imprisoned for debt when Charles was 12. Charles was forced to go to work in a blacking warehouse—an experience that fired his determination to fight his way out of poverty and influenced his lifelong efforts to alleviate the poor conditions in factories and mines.

When his father was released from prison, Charles finished school and went to work in an attorney's office. At 17, he fell in love with a banker's daughter, Maria Beadnell, but her family convinced her that he wasn't "good enough" for her. She was sent away to Europe, and Charles was devastated. His career plans changed, however, and by age 20 he had mastered a difficult shorthand system and had become a Parliamentary reporter. Under the pseudonym "Boz," Charles began writing street sketches that anticipate many of the themes later found in his novels: prisons, law courts, snobbery, and sympathy for the poor.

He married his editor's daughter, Catherine Hogarth, in 1836, and shortly thereafter published his first novel, *Pickwick Papers*, a narrative in numbered installments. He became an almost overnight, world-wide success. A prolific writer, he found that his rise in social importance kept pace with his literary fame. He founded and edited three periodicals in which his novels appeared in serialized form before being bound as books. His fiction was often critical of social conditions in England. The proceeds from dramatizations and readings of his work benefitted charities, and he worked with philanthropist Angela Coutts to establish a Home for Fallen Women.

In 1842, he and his wife traveled to the U.S., whose system of democracy he admired. He soon found that America was nearly as corrupt as England, however, and he angered many Americans by making them the targets of satire in *Martin Chuzzlewit*. By 1851, Charles' wife had borne him nine children, but in 1857, he began an affair with a young actress, Ellen Ternan, and his wife left him.

Ever restless, Charles made extensive tours and gave readings to augment his income—despite the fact that his health had been weakened by a terrible train wreck. Further debilitated by a lucrative but exhausting American tour, he suffered a stroke at dinner and died the next morning, June 9, 1870, at age 58.

Initiating Activities

Choose one or more of the following activities to establish an appropriate mindset for the story students are about to read.

1. Anticipation Guide: Students rate and discuss their opinions of statements which tap themes they will meet in the story.

   1 ——— 2 ——— 3 ——— 4 ——— 5 ——— 6

   agree strongly   strongly disagree

   _____ a. People get what they deserve, in the end.

   _____ b. You can never be too ambitious.

   _____ c. Dickens wrote about people and times that have little to do with me.

2. Video: Watch the 1935 black-and-white version of *Great Expectations* (with Lionel Barrymore, Maureen O'Sullivan, and W.C. Fields) released by MGM/United Artists Home Video and Turner Entertainment, 1990, in their Great Books on Video line (may be ordered from Novel Units).

3. Brainstorming: Have students generate associations with the word "infatuation," a theme that is central to the story, while a student scribe jots ideas around the central word on a large piece of paper or on the chalkboard. Help students "cluster" the ideas into categories. A sample framework is shown below.

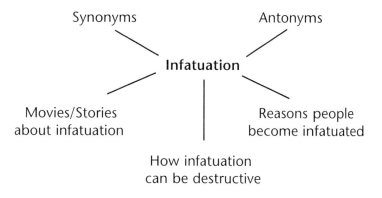

Synonyms   Antonyms

Infatuation

Movies/Stories   Reasons people
about infatuation   become infatuated

How infatuation
can be destructive

4. Geography: Have students examine or create a map showing the general setting of the story. Have them locate specific towns depicted in the story (Dover, Yarmouth, London, etc.).

5. Discussion:

   • Dickens' time: This is a long book (over 800 pages, with notes). What are some of the advantages that a long novel has over a shorter one? What can the author do that he doesn't have enough room for in a shorter version? *David Copperfield* was first presented in 19 installments. Of what modern type of entertainment does this remind you?

- Love: How would you define "love"? Is it possible to be in love with someone without knowing it? Are friendship and romantic love ever compatible? Could you think you were "just friends" with someone, and then later realize you were in love with him or her?
- Schools: What were schools like in Dickens' day? How were students treated? What sorts of punishments were meted out?

6. Prereading Research: Selected students (perhaps those in need of extra-credit points) should do some research on the following topics and report back to the whole group:

   a) prisons in Dickens' day (especially debtors' prisons)
   b) the British judicial system
   c) the British monetary system

7. Writing: Dickens wrote this novel when he was in his mid-thirties, and based it on many incidents and characters from his own life. Make a balloon-map of characters and incidents you would include in your own autobiography, looking back from the age you are now. (Use a framework like the one below, adding more balloons as necessary.)

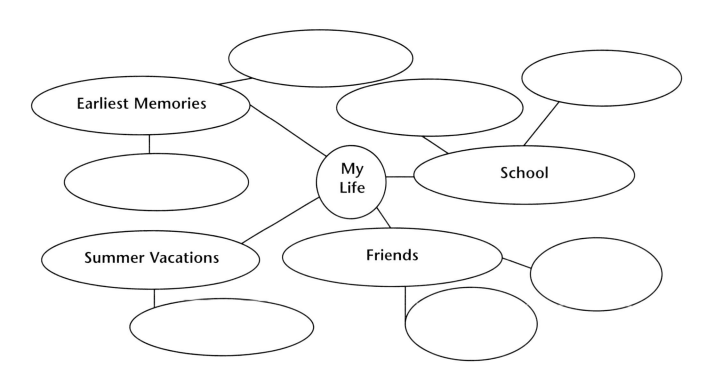

Using Predictions

We all make predictions as we read—little guesses about what will happen next, how a conflict will be resolved, which details will be important to the plot, which details will help fill in our sense of a character. Students should be encouraged to predict, to make sensible guesses as they read the novel.

As students work on their predictions, these discussion questions can be used to guide them: What are some of the ways to predict? What is the process of a sophisticated reader's thinking and predicting? What clues does an author give to help us make predictions? Why are some predictions more likely to be accurate than others?

Create a chart for recording predictions. This could be either an individual or class activity. As each subsequent chapter is discussed, students can review and correct their previous predictions about plot and characters as necessary.

Use the facts and ideas the author gives.

Use your own prior knowledge.

Apply any new information (i.e., from class discussion) that may cause you to change your mind.

Predictions

_____

_____

_____

_____

Prediction Chart

What characters have we met so far?	What is the conflict in the story?	What are your predictions?	Why did you make those predictions?

Using Character Webs

Attribute webs are simply a visual representation of a character from the novel. They provide a systematic way for students to organize and recap the information they have about a particular character. Attribute webs may be used after reading the novel to recapitulate information about a particular character, or completed gradually as information unfolds. They may be completed individually or as a group project.

One type of character attribute web uses these divisions:

- How a character acts and feels. (How does the character act? How do you think the character feels? How would you feel if this happened to you?)

- How a character looks. (Close your eyes and picture the character. Describe him/her to me.)

- Where a character lives. (Where and when does the character live?)

- How others feel about the character. (How does another specific character feel about our character?)

In group discussion about the characters described in student attribute webs, the teacher can ask for backup proof from the novel. Inferential thinking can be included in the discussion.

Attribute webs need not be confined to characters. They may also be used to organize information about a concept, object, or place.

Attribute Web

The attribute web below will help you gather clues the author provides about a character in the novel. Fill in the blanks with words and phrases which tell how the character acts and looks, as well as what the character says and what others say about him or her.

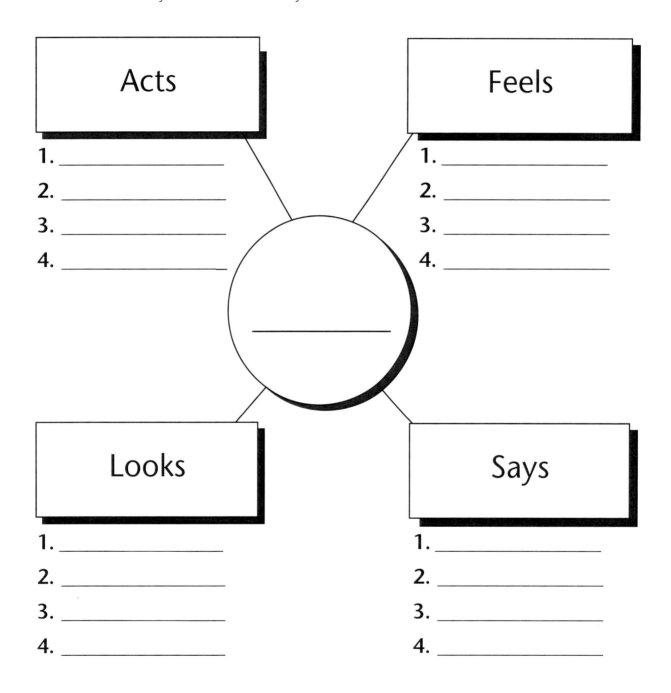

Acts

1. _____
2. _____
3. _____
4. _____

Feels

1. _____
2. _____
3. _____
4. _____

Looks

1. _____
2. _____
3. _____
4. _____

Says

1. _____
2. _____
3. _____
4. _____

Story Map

Characters _____

_____

Time and Place _____

_____

Problem _____

_____

_____

Goal _____

_____

_____

Beginning ⟶ Development ⟶ Outcome

_____

_____

_____

_____

Resolution _____

_____

_____

_____

Setting

Problem

Goal

Episodes

Resolution

Chapters I-VI

Vocabulary

caul 1	impiety 2	magnate 2	fender 5
rooks 5	annuity 8	propitiation 9	perspicuously 15
aspersion 18	broached 24	expostulate 25	sumptuous 29
inveterate 41	magnanimous 47	stoical 53	repudiated 60
expediency 64	almshouses 68	dromedary 75	viands 79

Context Definitions

There are many unfamiliar words in *David Copperfield*. Time-consuming vocabulary activities tend to negatively influence students' enjoyment of the story and perceptions of the author's style. One approach is to encourage students to develop context definitions as they read. This will not always be possible, but it will reduce the number of words to be looked up in a dictionary. In the list above, for instance, students will be able to deduce that "rooks" are some type of bird from Miss Betsey's question, "Where are the birds?—the rooks?" One can infer that a "fender" is a place where one might rest one's feet, and is near a fire. Knowing exactly what rooks or fenders look like is not important to an understanding of the story. Words whose meanings are not readily definable from context can be noted, and students can work in groups to quickly find and share dictionary definitions.

Discussion Questions

1. How long had David's father been dead when he was born? *(six months)* Why did his great aunt depart shortly after his birth? *(She was disappointed because he was not a girl and could not be named after her.)*

2. What are some of David's earliest memories? *(the house, a spooky storeroom, church pews, the garden, the kindness of his mother and Peggotty, Peggotty's buttons flying off)*

3. How do Peggotty and David feel about the first visit of the man with the black hair and beard? *(David feels jealous and uncomfortable; Peggotty tells Clara that her dead husband wouldn't like the man. Clara is offended and upset, and everyone ends up crying.)*

4. What is the joke about Brooks of Sheffield? *(Murdstone tells Quinion not to refer to "the pretty little widow," because of someone [David] being "sharp." He then pretends he's referring to Brooks of Sheffield, a famous maker of blades, but he and Quinion are actually talking about David and his lack of understanding of Murdstone's plans to marry Clara.)* Did you find it cruel of the men to make fun of David and to wish him "confusion"?

5. What example of foreshadowing do you find at the end of Chapter 2? *(On the eve of David's departure for Yarmouth, he says it now touches him "to think how little I suspected what I did leave forever.")* What could that mean?

6. How is the mood in Yarmouth different from that in Blunderstone? *(As Mr. Peggotty says, "You'll find us rough, but you'll find us ready." The mood is decidedly more joyful and relaxed than at Blunderstone. David has playmates and falls in love with Little Em'ly; he is enchanted with the whimsical boat where the Peggottys live, and where he stays.)*

7. What adjectives would you use to describe Mr. Peggotty? *(He is "a diamond in the rough"— hard-working, warm, generous and kind; Ham and Em'ly are orphans he has taken in as his own.)*

8. Who is Mrs. Gummidge? *(the widow of Mr. Peggotty's former partner)* Have you ever known a "lone, lorn creature" like her? Why do you suppose Dickens included her as a minor character in the novel? *(She is one of Dickens' classic humorous characters, and she serves that purpose well.)*

9. What surprise is waiting for David back home? *(Mr. Murdstone and his mother are now married.)* How does David's experience at the dog-kennel parallel his feelings about Mr. Murdstone? *(The dog, who is large and black and hairy like Murdstone, springs out of the kennel to "get at" David, who fears Murdstone.)*

10. How does Murdstone greet David? *(with warnings that if he doesn't obey he will be beaten)* How might he have acted differently, and what effect would that have had on David?

11. What words does Dickens choose to characterize Miss Murdstone and her possessions (pages 43-44)? *(gloomy, dark, heavy, hard black boxes, hard brass nails, hard steel purse, heavy chain, metallic)*

12. How do things change at Blunderstone after the arrival of Miss Murdstone? *(She plans to run the household her way; at first Clara protests, but then submits.)*

13. Why does David have so much trouble with his lessons? *(He learns them fine, but is so intimidated by the Murdstones that he is unable to remember when the time comes to recite.)* Have you ever felt this way? If you were a friend of David's what advice would you have given him?

14. How is the book collection left by David's father helpful to him? *(The books help him escape to fantasy worlds, and give him hope of escaping the circumstances of his present life.)*

15. How does David "fall into disgrace"? *(When Murdstone begins to beat David, David bites his hand.)* What are some possible consequences that concern David? *(He wonders if he has committed a criminal act and will be sent to prison, or be hanged.)* What does happen? *(He is kept in his room for five days.)* Does this seem like cruel and unusual punishment to you? Is it ever acceptable for an adult to beat a child? Did David have the right to defend himself?

16. How is Peggotty especially comforting to David perhaps more so than his mother? *(Unlike Clara, Peggotty lets David know how much she loves him and that he can always count on her. She catches up with the cart that takes him away to school, bringing him cakes and some money.)*

17. How does Barkis relieve the dramatic tension? *(Barkis, the cart-driver, lends humor to a sad situation with his cryptic marriage proposal, "Barkis is willin'!")*

18. How is David tricked by the waiter at the Inn? *(He tells David the ale could be deadly, then proceeds to drink it himself, then eats most of the rest of the meal to counter the bad effects of the ale. He also overcharges David for letter paper and wheedles a large tip from him.)*

19. What is Salem House like? *(run-down and dirty)* What embarrassment is waiting for David? *(He must wear a placard that says, "Take care of him. He bites.")* Who is Mr. Mell? *(the schoolmaster who picked David up in Whitechapel; Mell treated David kindly.)*

20. Besides looking rather like a monster, what is impressive about Mr. Creakle? *(He speaks only in a whisper.)*

21. With whom does David make friends? *(Tommy Traddles and J. Steerforth)* Do you think Steerforth takes advantage of David? *(He takes his money "for safekeeping," then convinces him to spend it on things Steerforth would like.)* Why is David so in awe of Steerforth? *(He sees him as a powerful figure, capable of protecting him.)*

22. **Prediction:** Will David be happier at Salem House than he was at home?

Author's Craft

Dickens was famous for inventing names for his characters which "matched" their traits. For example, Ham is a big, meaty sort of person and the Murdstones are like murderers with hearts of stone. Think about the names Mrs. Gummidge, Mr. Creakle, and Steerforth. What do these names make you think of? How do they match their characters?

Writing Idea

Write the conversation Mr. Murdstone and Mr. Creakle had when Murdstone arranged to have David attend Salem House School. Be sure to include Murdstone's special instructions for David's treatment, and Creakle's reactions.

Chapters VII-XII

Vocabulary

exordium 82	beadle 84	bruited 87	contrition 93
prodigious 95	infantine 100	actuate 105	efficacious 106
obdurate 109	diabolical 119	unamiable 119	imperturbable 119
sagacious 126	draughts 132	languished 138	oscillating 141
emulation 143	peregrinations 144	disparity 151	improvident 158

Discussion Questions

1. What seems to be Creakle's chief joy in life? *(caning the boys)* Why is there very little real learning taking place? *(The boys are too worried and frightened to concentrate.)*

2. Traddles took the beating when Steerforth laughed in church, and his reward was that Steerforth proclaimed there was nothing of the sneak in him. What does this tell you about Steerforth? about the other boys? *(Steerforth could have stepped forward and saved Traddles; the other boys all seem to be duped by him.)*

3. How does David—sometimes very wearily—entertain the boys? *(He tells the stories he learned so well from his father's book collection.)*

4. What were the "unforeseen consequences" of David's visit with Mr. Mell to the almshouse where his mother lived? *(David had told Steerforth about the visit, and when Mr. Mell tried to correct Steerforth during class, Steerforth used his knowledge about the almshouse to embarrass Mr. Mell, who was then fired by Creakle.)*

5. Why does Mr. Mell feel so differently about Steerforth than the boys do? *(As an adult, he clearly sees how Steerforth uses the others and that Steerforth has a position of favoritism which allows him to get away with anything.)* Why do you suppose Creakle is so partial to Steerforth?

6. Who comes to visit David and what do they bring? *(Ham and Mr. Peggotty come, bringing lots of the seafood that David loves.)* How do they react to Steerforth? *(They immediately like him, and invite him to visit them in Yarmouth.)*

7. On his arrival back at Blunderstone for the holidays, who does David meet? *(his baby brother)* How is it that David spends one happy afternoon at home? *(The Murdstones are out and not expected back before night. David, Peggotty, and Clara spend the afternoon together.)*

8. How have the Murdstones exerted their influence over Clara? *(She now sees their domination as devotion and defends them and their intentions.)*

9. How does David spend the holidays? *(sitting miserably in the parlor, at Murdstone's direction)* What would he have preferred? *(to take refuge in his room or with Peggotty)*

10. What hints are there in Chapter 8 that David's mother will die soon? *(Clara asks Peggotty to take care of her and says, "It will not be for long, perhaps" [p. 102]; "...that evening, as the last of its race, an destined evermore to close that volume of my life" [p. 106]; "So I lost her" [p. 112].)*

11. How does the news of his mother's death affect David? *(He is "stricken with sincere grief.")* Why does he stop off in Yarmouth on his way home? *(to be fitted for a suit for the mourning period)*

12. How does David get through the days before and after the funeral? *(Peggotty is his comfort and consolation.)*

13. What parallel does the author draw between David's dead brother and himself? *(David feels he is saying goodbye to a time when he felt all his mother's love and goodness. The child who experienced those things is now as dead as his brother.)*

14. What plans and promises does Peggotty make after Clara's death? *(After the Murdstones tell her she is no longer needed, she plans to go to Yarmouth; she promises to come and see David once a week, but first she gets permission to take him with her for a visit.)*

15. Do you think Peggotty really wants to marry Barkis, or is that just the easiest thing to do at the moment? *(Answers will vary.)*

16. How is the situation at Yarmouth different than it was on David's last visit? *(Em'ly is busy learning how to be a little woman; she often teases David.)*

17. How do the Murdstone's treat David on his return to Blunderstone? *(They neglect and ignore him.)* Is this treatment better or worse than the way they acted before?

18. What do you think is Murdstone's main reason for sending David away to work at the warehouse? *(He probably just wants him out of the way; he certainly has no interest in how David turns out.)* What do you suppose happened to the Copperfield properties? *(Murdstone apparently inherited everything from Clara.)*

19. With whom does David lodge in London? *(the Micawbers)* What are they like? *(Mr. Micawber is quite eloquent; he has a faded wife and four children. His creditors are always at the door demanding money.)*

20. What is David's chief physical problem while he is in London? *(He is always hungry.)* his chief emotional problem? *(He feels hopeless, abandoned, and different from the others who work at the warehouse)*

21. How do the Micawbers enlist David's help in their financial matters and then reward him? *(They send him to the pawnbroker with various possessions, then have him join them for supper.)*

22. What is so ludicrous about David's situation? *(At 10, he is expected to act like an adult.)* Are children today ever expected to act as responsibly as David must?

23. How does King's Bench Prison compare to modern prisons in this country? *(The inmates live in rooms rather than cells; their families often live with them.)*

24. What phrase summarizes Mr. Micawber's hope for the future? *("Something will turn up.")*

25. While he was in prison, what did Mr. Micawber prepare to be sent to the House of Commons? *(a petition to change the laws regarding imprisonment for debt)* Does it make sense, do you think, to put someone in prison for debt? Does it ever happen today?

26. What does Mrs. Micawber promise? *(that she will never desert Mr. Micawber)*

27. What decision does David make, and what happens because of it? *(David decides to run away to his Aunt Betsey Trotwood's in Dover. He is robbed of all his money and clothing.)*

28. **Prediction:** Will David be able to get to his aunt's house, or will some other tragedy befall him in the mean time? If he does get there, how will he be received?

Chalkboard Activity

Several probable causes lead to the death of David's mother. In turn, her death has certain important effects on David's and Peggotty's lives. Use a framework like the one on the following page to review the cause-effect relationships noted, eliciting input from students. Use the same organizer to trace cause-and-effect correlations between other events later in the novel.

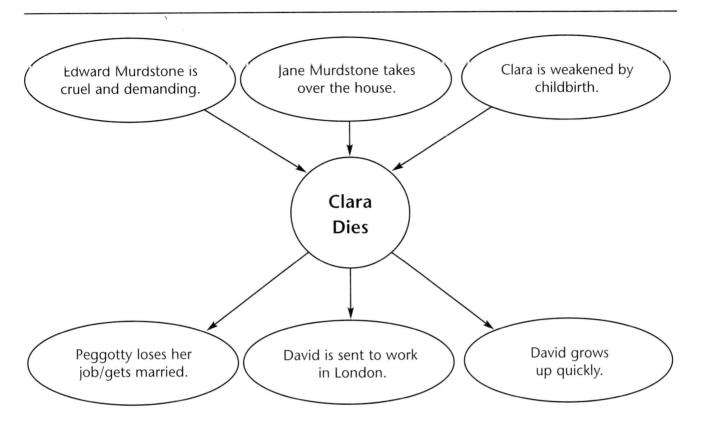

Chapters XIII-XVII

Vocabulary

jocose 174	destitute 174	restoratives 177	abjuration 179
decried 182	beseech 183	alacrity 186	amenable 189
habiliments 190	irascibility 194	odious 197	cadaverous 201
nankeen 203	sublimated 208	spectre 215	cogitating 219
reticule 227	chary 230	pecuniary 239	approbation 241

Discussion Questions

1. How do David's experiences of going to the pawnbroker for the Micawbers help him out in Chapter 13? *(It occurs to him to sell his clothes.)* If you filmed the scene at the second shop—Charley's—would you film it as a funny incident, or would you focus on David's fear? How would you film David's encounters with the trampers and tinkers?

2. What is Miss Betsey's first reaction to David? *("Go away! No boys here!" She thinks he is a beggar.)* Once his identity is made known, what does Mr. Dick advise Miss Betsey to do? *(wash him)*

3. Who is Janet, and what is Miss Betsey trying to teach her? *(She works as a servant; Miss Betsey is trying to teach her to renounce men.)* What might Miss Betsey's reasons be for being so against men?

4. What crisis occurs regularly at Miss Betsey's? *(Donkeys come into the yard and must be chased away.)*

5. Judging from David's remarks at the end of Chapter 13, how do you suppose Dickens would react to the current problem of homelessness?

6. When Miss Betsey refers to David's father-in-law, who does she mean, and what term is used today? *(Mr. Murdstone; stepfather)* Are you surprised that she contacted him?

7. How does Mr. Dick pass the time? *(by writing a Memorial)* What problem keeps him from finishing it? *(King Charles the First keeps popping up. Mr. Dick doesn't want him in the Memorial, so he starts over.)* Do you think Mr. Dick is out of his mind? Does Miss Betsey think he is?

8. How does Miss Betsey greet the Murdstones? *(Since they arrive on donkeys, she rushes out to chase them away, not realizing who they are. Even after David informs her, she continues to rail at them.)*

9. Do you think Murdstone really wants to take David with him? What are Miss Betsey's reasons for keeping him with her? *(She quickly surmises that Murdstone stole David's rightful inheritance and hastened Clara's death by breaking her heart; Mr. Dick advises having David measured for a suit.)*

10. How does Miss Betsey insult Miss Murdstone? *(by ignoring her)*

11. What new name does David acquire? *(Trotwood Copperfield)*

12. Who is Uriah Heep and what is he like? *(Mr. Wickfield's assistant, Uriah, is cadaverous-looking, with short-cropped red hair, hardly any eyebrows and no lashes, and a bony and skeleton-like frame.)*

13. What is the atmosphere like at Mr. Wickfield's? *(Aside from the presence of ghostly Uriah, the house is pleasant, quiet, and comfortable. Mr. Wickfield's daughter, Agnes, is devoted to her father.)*

14. Why does David feel alienated at Canterbury? *(He has experienced much more of "real life" than his schoolmates, yet is put in the lowest form because he has not learned much in the academic sense.)*

15. How does David feel about Agnes? *(She represents goodness, peace, and truth for him.)*

16. What adjective does Uriah insist applies to himself? *(humble)* Do you think his repetition of this word is irritating? Do you think he has ulterior motives?

17. Who is Jack Maldon? *(the cousin of Dr. Strong's young wife, Annie)* Before his departure for India, Annie "loses" one of her ribbons. Where do you think it is?

18. What clue to the content of Chapter 17 is there in its title? *("Somebody Turns Up" is a variation of Mr. Micawber's favorite expression, "something will turn up.")*

19. What was especially uncomfortable about David's visit with Uriah and his mother? *(They wormed things out of him that he didn't want to tell.)* Who comes along to "save" him? *(Mr. Micawber)* What are his plans? *(to go into the coal trade)*

20. How does the rapidly changeable nature of Micawber's life show itself in this section? *(He writes David a letter saying all is lost; the next day David sees the family riding in a coach, looking quite happy.)*

21. **Prediction:** Who is the man in the yard to whom Mr. Dick has seen Aunt Betsey giving money? Is it simply a delusion, or could it have something to do with her negative feelings toward men?

Chalkboard Activity

Use a Venn diagram to compare and contrast Dr. Strong and Mr. Creakle. Common characteristics should go in the overlapping area; unique traits go in the respective names' circles.

Dr. Strong   **Mr. Creakle**

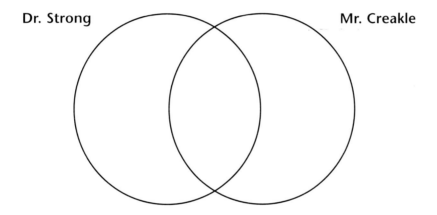

Writing Idea

Before leaving him at the Wickfield's, Aunt Betsey gives David some advice: never be mean, false, or cruel in anything. Do you think this advice is all one needs to get along in life? What other advice would you add if you were sending your child off to school?

Chapters XVIII-XXIII

Vocabulary

propitious 245	brazier 252	evince 261	ignoble 267
profligacy 270	altercation 272	pliant 275	portmanteaus 277
rheumatics 283	capricious 297	nautical 298	smiting 304
volatile 307	volubility 307	proctor 315	solicitor 315
ecclesiastical 316	advocates 316	laudable 317	audacity 318

© Novel Units, Inc.

21

Discussion Questions

1. What are David's early experiences with romance? *(He falls quickly in love, and just as quickly out of love, with Miss Shepherd; then he develops a crush on an older woman, Miss Larkins, who promptly gets married.)* Do you think he acts foolish, or is this the kind of thing everyone goes through in their teens?

2. David has a difficult time thinking of anything he wants to do with his life. What advice does his aunt give him? *(She wants him to develop strength of character and self-reliance—as she has. She suggests he take a little trip and think things over.)*

3. What promise does David make to Agnes? *(that he will always tell her when he is in trouble or in love)*

4. What is troubling Agnes as she and David say goodbye? *(She is concerned that her father is beginning to act very nervous, and that Uriah has something to do with whatever is wrong.)*

5. What do you think could be the reason for Mr. Wickfield's objection to the friendship between Agnes and Annie? *(Answers will vary.)*

6. How do David's efforts to seem mature and sophisticated backfire immediately? *(He is easily intimidated by a man named William into giving up his seat on the coach.)*

7. Do you think Steerforth is as glad to see David as David is to see him? *(David is so delighted that he sheds a few tears; Steerforth is more casual and acts in a big-brotherly but slightly condescending way, giving David the nickname of Daisy. He tells David he wants to hear all about him because he feels as if David were his "property.")*

8. What is Steerforth's home like? *(It is a stately brick house on a hill in Highgate; both the house and Steerforth's mother are very genteel.)*

9. Who is Rosa Dartle? What does she look like? How does she act? *(She is Mrs. Steerforth's companion, a dark-haired woman of about 30 with a large scar on her lip. She corrects every statement, and asks for more information in every conversation.)*

10. What is Steerforth's comment about the Peggottys and "that sort of people"? *(page 271; "…there's a pretty wide separation between them and us. They are not to be expected to be as sensitive as we are.")* How does David react to this statement? *(He can't believe Steerforth has made such a remark in seriousness.)*

11. How did Rosa Dartle get the scar on her lip? *(Steerforth threw a hammer at her long ago.)* Does Steerforth seem to bear any guilt for his past actions? *(no)*

12. Do you think Mrs. Steerforth's bragging about her son's attributes is in poor taste? Does David find it unpleasant, or does he enjoy it? *(He enjoys it.)*

13. Does Littimer remind you of anyone you have seen in a movie? *(He is the classic stiff valet seen in many movies and in numerous PBS productions about the Victorian English, i.e., Upstairs, Downstairs.)* How does Littimer make David feel? *(very young)*

14. When David and Steerforth arrive in Yarmouth, what information does Mr. Omer volunteer about Emily? *(There was a rumor going around that Emily wanted to be "a lady," and that she held herself above others; now it seems that she has accepted her position in life, and she works for Omer.)*

15. Why is it "the brightest of nights" at Mr. Peggotty's? *(Emily and Ham have announced they plan to be married.)* Is the night as bright for David? *(He feels a little sensitive about it, having been half in love with Emily for so long.)*

16. Why do Steerforth's comments about the Peggottys, particularly Ham, surprise David? *(David is genuinely fond of all his Yarmouth friends; Steerforth had seemed warm and friendly to them, but his remarks about them being "quaint company" and Ham being "a chuckleheaded fellow" seem to indicate that it's all just an amusement to Steerforth.)*

17. In Chapter 22, David sees Steerforth in rare, low spirits. Is there any indication what has caused such a mood? Can you find any clues in the text? *(Answers will vary.)*

18. What great favor has Steerforth done Mr. Peggotty? *(Steerforth has bought a boat, christened it The Little Em'ly, and asked Mr. Peggotty to captain it in his absence.)*

19. Who is Miss Mowcher? *(a dwarf, about 45, who administers various beauty treatments as she travels around the country)* Why do you think Dickens included her? *(She appears here for comic relief, but will reappear later in a more important role.)*

20. What does Steerforth tell Miss Mowcher about Emily? *(that she is throwing herself away and was meant to be a lady)* Do you think he has any plans regarding Emily?

21. Who is Martha, and why is Emily talking to her secretly? *(Martha is a "fallen woman," but she and Emily were friends when Martha worked at Omer's, and Emily kindly gives her some money.)*

22. Why do you think Emily gets so upset about not being a "better girl" and not being thankful enough for Ham? *(Answers will vary.)*

23. Back in London, what career does David enter upon? *(He will study to be a proctor, or ecclesiastical attorney, at the suggestion of his aunt and with the approval of Steerforth.)*

24. On the way to Spenlow and Jorkins, Aunt Betsey becomes very upset by the sight of a poorly-dressed man, who she then goes off with, alone, for a few minutes. What do you think this mystery is about? *(Answers will vary.)*

25. What function does Mr. Jorkins seem to perform for the firm of Spenlow and Jorkins? *(Jorkins is blamed for "fettering" an otherwise kindly Spenlow; in actuality Jorkins is mild-mannered and has little to do with the business.)*

26. What is your impression of Doctors Commons? Does it seem like the sort of place you would like to work? *(Answers will vary.)*

27. How does Mrs. Crupp, David's new landlady, ease any anxiety David and Aunt Betsey might have had about his being on his own? *(She says she will treat David like a son and take good*

care of him.) Do you see any possible disadvantages for David in having a landlady with her attitude?

28. **Prediction:** On page 286, David says of Steerforth, "If anyone had told me, then, that all this was a brilliant game, played for the excitement of the moment, for the employment of high spirits, in the thoughtless love of superiority, in a mere wasteful careless course of winning what was worthless to him, and next minute thrown away: I say, if any one had told me such a lie that night, I wonder in what manner of receiving it my indignation would have found a vent!" What course of events do you think is being foreshadowed in this passage?

Writing Ideas

1. When David first sees Yarmouth after a long absence, he feels it is smaller than when he was there previously. Write about a place to which you returned after a long absence, describing your impressions and feelings.

2. Write a character sketch of someone you admire who is a little older than you, someone who acts like a big brother or sister. What qualities would you like to emulate? Does the person have any obvious faults?

Chapters XXIV-XXX

Vocabulary

commodious 330	expiate 334	deplorable 335	ascendancy 340
deference 342	desultory 344	recompense 353	phaeton 355
interrogatory 356	delirium 361	maudlin 361	vexatious 363
gout 371	curate 372	salubrity 374	perfidy 377
phrenologically 380	comestibles 380	encomiums 383	countenance 403

Discussion Questions

1. Describe David's "first dissipation." *(David has a party with Steerforth and his two friends, and becomes very inebriated. They all go to the theatre, and unfortunately Agnes is there and witnesses David's drunken behavior.)*

2. Why does David make so many attempts at his letter of reply to Agnes? *(He feels very ashamed that she saw him in such terrible shape, and no words he can think of seem adequate to express his feelings.)*

3. Does Agnes blame David for getting drunk? *(no)* What warning does she give him? *(She tells him that she feels Steerforth is a "dangerous friend.")*

4. What problem is bothering Agnes? *(Uriah Heep seems to have attained a kind of power over her father, and it looks as though they will become partners.)*

5. What did Dickens mean by, "We were so exceedingly genteel that our scope was very limited"? *(Most topics were considered too vulgar to be discussed by this excessively snobbish group of people.)*

6. Who happens to be at the Waterbrooks' dinner party? *(Tommy Traddles)* Do you think this coincidence is a little too convenient, or is it believable?

7. What disturbing confession does Uriah make to David? *(He is in love with Agnes and hopes to marry her one day.)*

8. Explain the title of Chapter 26, "I Fall Into Captivity." *(When David meets Dora Spenlow, he falls madly and completely in love.)*

9. Who has been hired as Dora's companion? *(Miss Murdstone)* Does this bother David? *(He is jealous of anyone who spends time with Dora. At least he is able, as an adult, to tell Miss Murdstone exactly what he thinks of her.)*

10. What do you think of Dora? What are her limitations and strengths? *(Although Dora is the classic "airhead," she is cheerful and beautiful.)* Does she remind you of anyone you know?

11. What does David learn about Tommy Traddles' past? *(Traddles was brought up by an uncle who didn't care much about him; when the uncle married and then died, his young widow got most of his money.)* What are Traddles' plans for the future? *(He will continue to study law and hopes to get ahead in the world; he is engaged.)*

12. Knowing Traddles' seeming attraction to misfortune, do you think he will ever marry Sophy? *(Answers will vary.)*

13. What additional coincidence comes to light during David's visit with Traddles? *(Traddles boards with the Micawbers.)*

14. Has Micawber changed much? *(As usual, he is having a temporary setback, waiting to spring forward into some great opportunity, as soon as "something turns up.")*

15. How does David's dinner party turn out? *(It would have been a failure, except that the people in attendance are all such good friends; they cook the meat on a gridiron, stir up some sauce, and have a good time.)*

16. Do you find the appearance of Littimer, and his behavior, strange? Does David feel something is wrong? *(page 382, "…my conscience had embarrassed me with whispers that I had mistrusted his master.")*

17. Do Steerforth's remarks about Traddles and Barkis surprise you? *(Answers will vary.)*

18. How has Traddles gotten himself into trouble on account of Mr. Micawber? *(He loaned Micawber money, and now the repayment is not going to be made.)*

19. How does Rosa Dartle treat David when he goes to Highgate? *(She questions him about Steerforth's activities and implies that Steerforth and his mother are not getting along as well as usual.)* How does Steerforth succeed in making her angry? *(He jokingly tells her they can love one another forever, and she hits him and rushes out of the room.)*

20. Why does Mr. Omer say he smokes? *(for his asthma)* What advice would you give him?

21. To what do you attribute Emily's coldness and trembling on seeing David? Why do you think she seems to avoid Ham? *(Answers will vary.)*

22. What are Barkis' dying words? *("Barkis is willin'.")*

23. **Prediction:** Re-read the last sentence of Chapter 29. Consider this passage and Rosa Dartle's behavior, and use other clues to predict what you think will happen concerning Steerforth.

Writing Idea

Rosa Dartle is obviously in love with Steerforth, and he makes a joke of this. What do you think is the best way to act when you know someone is attracted to you, but you don't feel the same way? What do Steerforth's actions indicate about his character? What other characteristics of his are starting to become apparent?

Chapters XXXI-XXXVI

Vocabulary

remonstrance 413	inexorable 421	sedulously 421	equable 422
libertine 426	hapless 427	vehemence 434	conundrum 436
etherealised 436	antipathy 438	rankled 438	anomalies 440
sinecures 441	dotage 442	irrevocable 446	stipulated 449
dejected 459	conflagration 461	rapturous 464	umbrage 482

Discussion Questions

1. In all, how much money did Barkis leave to Peggotty, Mr. Peggotty, Little Em'ly, and David? *(3000 pounds)*

2. To what does the title, "A Greater Loss" refer? *(Em'ly has run away with Steerforth.)* How does David react? *(He feels responsible for causing the tragic event by bringing Steerforth to Yarmouth to visit; he chooses to think of Steerforth as dead.)* What does Mr. Peggotty plan to do? *(search until he finds Emily)*

3. What change is apparent in Mrs. Gummidge? *(She stops complaining and comforts Mr. Peggotty, advising him that he must eat something, and that she will always be there for him to depend on.)*

4. What does Miss Mowcher reveal to David? *(She was tricked into assisting in Steerforth's plans to be with Emily; she is especially angry at Littimer.)* What does she promise to do? *(to let David know immediately if she hears anything about the runaways)* Do you think Miss Mowcher will get her revenge on Littimer?

5. Who do David, Mr. Peggotty, and Peggotty go to see in London? *(Mrs. Steerforth)* What does she tell them? *(that Emily is beneath Steerforth and that the match is impossible)* How does she further insult Mr. Peggotty? *(by offering him money, as if she can buy her way out of an embarrassing situation)*

6. What is Rosa Dartle's reaction to the news about Steerforth and Emily? *(She calls the Peggottys "a depraved, worthless set" and says she would have Emily whipped.)*

7. Compare Mr. Peggotty's feelings toward Emily with those of Mrs. Steerforth toward her son. Who is obviously the more kind and forgiving? *(Mr. Peggotty)* What social statement do you think Dickens is making about the rich and the poor? *(A common theme in Dickens' work is that the rich are greedy, selfish, and cruel while the poor have hearts of gold and are kind and generous.)*

8. Who is applying for a marriage license at the Commons? *(Mr. Murdstone)* Who is he marrying? *(a young woman with money)* Why was David fairly polite to him? *(He felt it was not the place for recriminations.)*

9. Judging from what Dickens has to say in Chapter 33 about easy government jobs (sinecures), waste, and salaries, what do you think he would have to say about the United States' system of government today? *(The same weaknesses exist in our system.)*

10. Jip isn't described completely, although we do know he's a little dog. What breed do you think he is? Does it seem odd that Dora is so attached to him? *(Dora is very child-like, and her fascination with her dog is a good way to show this.)*

11. Who is Miss Mills, and in what way does she help David? *(Miss Mills, a friend of Dora's, tells David that Dora will be visiting her and he is welcome to come by to see her.)*

12. Do you think David really knows what love is? Does Dora? Are they old enough to be engaged? How are David's feelings about Agnes like or unlike those he has for Dora? *(See the beginning of Chapter 34 for several paragraphs about Agnes. David is fond of Agnes as a best friend or sister, while his feelings for Dora are of the head-over-heels-in-love variety.)*

13. Why is Mrs. Crupp angry at Peggotty? *(Peggotty's efficiency makes Mrs. Crupp look bad; she is jealous that Peggotty has taken over her duties as David's surrogate mother.)* What does Mrs. Crupp do in retaliation? *(She leaves things on the stairs in the hope that Peggotty will fall and break her legs.)*

14. To David's surprise, who is waiting for him when he and Traddles go up to his apartment? *(Aunt Betsey, Mr. Dick, two birds, and a cat)* Why are they there? *(Aunt Betsey has lost all her money, and has nowhere else to go.)*

15. Why does Aunt Betsey say to David, "...blind, blind, blind!" *(She sees his professed love for Dora as rather silly.)* Why do you think this phrase is repeated at the end of Chapter 35?

16. How does the change in Aunt Betsey's financial state affect David? *(He has terrible dreams about poverty and not being good enough for Dora; he tries to get back the money his aunt paid for him to be articled, to no avail.)*

17. What has been happening at the Wickfields? *(Uriah Heep is now Mr. Wickfield's partner, and he is "so much between" Agnes and her father that she has difficulty watching over him.)* What reasons do you suppose Heep has for wanting to keep Agnes and her father from being together too much?

18. How does David decide to help out financially? *(by becoming Dr. Strong's secretary and by learning shorthand to become a court reporter)*

19. In Chapter 36, how does Dickens again pick up his theme that the rich are insensitive to the suffering of the poor? *(Jack Maldon serves this purpose, page 483.)*

20. How will Mr. Dick "provide for Miss Trotwood"? *(copying legal documents)*

21. What job has Mr. Micawber obtained? *(confidential clerk to Uriah Heep)*

22. **Prediction:** Will Mr. Peggotty ever find Emily, or is he out of the story now?

Writing Activity

A **found poem** is a piece of already-written prose rearranged in poem form. Found poems can be in newspapers or magazines, on package labels, in textbooks, and especially in novels. On page 444 (Chapter 33), there is a particularly appropriate passage of prose that lends itself well to becoming a found poem. It is rearranged below.

> The sun shone Dora
> and the birds sang Dora.
> The south wind blew Dora
> and the wildflowers in the hedges were all Doras
> to a bud.

There are numerous other passages in this novel which are good candidates for being transformed into found poems. The most "poetic" passages are those containing metaphors and similes. Choose three passages and rearrange each into poem form.

Chapters XXXVII-XLIII

Vocabulary

graminivorous 494	felicity 494	supplication 497	depravity 505
mercenary 509	fallacious 512	renunciation 517	inveigler 518
stipendiary 520	emoluments 520	clandestine 524	fatuity 533
inclement 539	inestimable 544	trepidation 547	concurrence 553
self-laudation 559	incumbent 567	perambulations 575	infidel 578

Discussion Questions

1. How did Aunt Betsey deal with Mrs. Crupp? *(Mrs. Crupp became convinced Aunt Betsey was insane when Aunt Betsey decided to throw the pitchers left on the stair to trip her and began prowling around in her bonnet as if hunting down Mrs. Crupp.)*

2. Why has David decided to throw himself into his several kinds of work with such energy? *(David makes a kind of deal with himself, that he will "deserve" Dora by being an extremely hard worker.)*

3. David explains to Dora that "a crust well-earned is sweeter far than a feast inherited." Do you agree with him, or would you prefer inheriting someone else's wealth to earning a modest living on your own? *(Answers will vary.)*

4. What does David try to tell Dora, as gently as possible, about their future together? *(He encourages her to think of him as a poor man and to try to learn a little about cooking and housekeeping.)* What is Dora's reaction? *(She doesn't want to think about what David is telling her, so she faints.)* Do you find yourself liking Dora, hating her, or simply viewing her as a comic character? What do you see about her that David seems blind to?

5. Does David find it easy to learn shorthand? *(no)* Why does he want to learn it? *(He wants to become a reporter on proceedings in Parliament.)* How would his task be made easier today? *(tape recorder, video recorder, court reporting machine)*

6. How does the evil Miss Murdstone once again make David's life miserable? *(She finds his letters to Dora and gives them to Mr. Spenlow, who confronts David with them.)*

7. What deal does David make with Mr. Spenlow? *(David at first refuses to "forget about" Dora; when Spenlow pressures him, he agrees to take a week to think about it. Spenlow makes it clear he will send Dora abroad if David persists in his intentions to marry her.)*

8. What very convenient coincidence occurs shortly after David's conference with Mr. Spenlow? *(Mr. Spenlow dies.)* What is surprising about Spenlow's financial situation? *(He spent more than he earned, and Dora is almost penniless.)* Where will Dora go now? *(to Putney, to live with two aunts)* Knowing what you do about Dickens' own life, do you think he enjoyed having Spenlow die, and then portraying him in this light?

9. To what might you compare the system of inveigling? *(personal injury attorneys who track down accident victims and initiate large lawsuits in their names)*

10. How does Mr. Micawber describe Mr. Wickfield? *(obsolete)* In what way does Micawber seem changed? *(He is secretive about the work he is doing for Uriah Heep.)*

11. What does Mr. Micawber mean about the letters "D" and "A"? *(He was surprised about David's feelings for Dora. He had supposed David would end up with Agnes.)* Why do you think David had such strong feelings of déja vu when Micawber said this?

12. How did Agnes help David out of his depression over Dora? *(by suggesting he contact her aunts and ask their permission to visit Dora)* Who interferes with their opportunity to have much of a conversation? *(Mrs. Heep, who is constantly with them and talks incessantly)*

13. How does David relieve Uriah's mind? *(by telling him he's engaged to someone other than Agnes)*

14. Although Mr. Wickfield has grown quite subservient to Uriah Heep, what causes him to go almost insane with anger? *(Heep's statement that he would like to marry Agnes)* Has Wickfield really been unaware of Heep's takeover? *(Wickfield confesses that he has let his emotions and his grief over the loss of his wife cause him to lose track of things and let Heep take over.)*

15. What does David ask Agnes to promise him? *(that she will not sacrifice herself because of a sense of duty, i.e., marry Heep to protect her father's business)*

16. When David meets up with Mr. Peggotty in London, what does he learn about Emily? *(She has been in Europe, has sent several letters containing money and asking for forgiveness, but makes it clear she can never come home.)* Who is secretly listening? *(Martha Endell)* Why do you think she doesn't come forward? Where is Mr. Peggotty going now? *(to a town on the Upper Rhine, where he believes Emily may be)*

17. Why is David upset that Julia Mills is going to India with her father? *(Julia, as foolish and romantic as David, has been a great help to him in delivering messages, talking things over, and assuring him he is on the right course.)*

18. Do you think Dickens' comparison of Dora's aunts to birds is an effective one? Does it help you to picture them? How do you imagine them talking, walking, sitting? *(Answers will vary.)*

19. What promise do the aunts extract from David? *(that there will be no secret communications between him and Dora)*

20. How is Dora's treatment of Jip very much like everyone's treatment of Dora herself? *(Both are indulged and regarded as playthings who needn't amount to much.)* How does Dora react when David points out that she should be treated "rationally"? *(She pouts and cries.)*

21. What situation does Uriah Heep feel compelled to point out to Dr. Strong and how does he get David involved? *(Heep says that Annie, Dr. Strong's young wife, is "much too sweet" on her cousin, Jack Maldon, who is now back from India and around quite a lot. He says David has noticed it too.)*

22. Dr. Strong's reaction to Heep's information is rather unusual—in what way? *(He blames himself for marrying such a young woman and realizes she is probably bored.)*

23. Why does David finally lash out and slap Uriah? *(He has never liked Uriah, and being trapped into the incident at Dr. Strong's is the final straw.)*

24. What does Mrs. Micawber write to David? *(that Mr. Micawber has distanced himself from the family)* How do you explain this situation?

25. At 21, what has David accomplished in his career and personal life? *(He now writes for the newspaper, and is regularly paid for magazine articles; He and Dora are married.)* Why did Dickens choose the present tense to relate David's memories of the wedding (Chapter 43)? *(Use of the present tense adds to the fairy-tale, dreamlike mood of this chapter by allowing the reader to experience it in a you-are-there-too mode.)*

26. **Prediction:** Do you think Dora will give up her childish ways and be able to manage a household?

Writing Idea

Imagine you are Dora. Write the letter she sends to her friend, Julia, a few days before the wedding. Try to capture Dora's personality in your letter, and include some details about her daily life to add realism to your letter.

Chapters XLIV-XLIX

Vocabulary

piquet 591	immolation 594	pretence 598	inducement 601
inviolable 604	absolves 608	disparity 610	munificence 611
lurid 615	obeisance 616	ineffaceable 621	cumbered 627
inauspiciously 627	privation 634	penitent 638	emissary 639
severance 647	sardonically 653	mountebank 656	aversion 657

Discussion Questions

1. David finds it strange that Dora is now always there, as if romance has been put away on a shelf. Do you think this always happens when people get married, or does it only happen if the relationship is shallow to begin with? *(Answers will vary.)*

2. Does Mary Anne Paragon turn out to be true to her last name? *(No; She is inefficient and steals money and silverware.)*

3. Did you find the chapter on housekeeping difficulties funny or serious? *(The washerwoman pawning the clothes, Jip walking on the table, the tipsy servant, the deformed sheep are all classic dry Dickens wit—but of course, the situation was quite serious to David and Dora!)* What advice would you give Dora if you were her neighbor or friend? If you were David, how would you deal with Dora?

4. How does David finally resolve his difficulties with Dora? *(He decides to solve the household problems himself.)* Do you think he is less in love with her than he was before the marriage? Can you be disappointed in someone, but still be in love with them?

5. In what ways does Dora prove true to the name she requests David use for her, "child-wife"? *(She says she is trying to "be good," begs David "don't send me to bed," wants to hold the pens while he is working.)*

6. How does Mr. Dick prove that Aunt Betsey was right about him being an exemplary fellow? *(Mr. Dick is concerned about the deterioration of the Strongs' marriage. He urges them to talk together and resolve the difficulties instituted by Uriah Heep.)*

7. How does Mrs. Markleham finally get her "just due"? *(Annie admits she was young and innocent when she first married Dr. Strong, and that she was urged into the marriage by her mother, who saw in it the potential for financial gain.)*

8. How does Annie clarify an incident from earlier in the novel? *(She refers to the night Jack Maldon left for India, explaining that he had made advances to her with the idea that she had*

married the doctor only for money and would be receptive to an affair with him. Annie, highly offended, has not spoken to him since.)

9. What news of Emily does David gain from Rosa Dartle and Littimer? *(Steerforth and Emily quarreled frequently, and Steerforth left her with the implication that she should now marry Littimer. A nearly suicidal Emily escaped from Littimer, and hasn't been heard from since.)*

10. How did Littimer both profit and lose from his association with Steerforth? *(Littimer was hurt by Steerforth's actions, and is now unemployed, however he was able to sell his information to Mrs. Steerforth.)*

11. What is meant by "...before I looked upon those two again, a stormy sea had risen to their feet" (page 622)? *(Answers will vary.)*

12. Why does David feel so sure Emily will contact Martha if she comes back to London? *(Like Emily, Martha is in disgrace and has no friends because of it. Emily was once kind to Martha, giving her money so she could leave Yarmouth.)*

13. What is Martha's present occupation? *(She is apparently a prostitute.)* What is her state of mind? *(When Mr. Peggotty and David find her, she is about to drown herself in the river.)*

14. What has been Martha's worst fear since hearing about Emily's disappearance? *(that people would think Emily had been corrupted by her association with Martha)*

15. The mystery of the man who sometimes demands money from Aunt Betsey is finally solved. Who is he? *(her husband, who turned out to be a gambler and a cheat)* Why do you think she has decided to tell David the story of her disastrous marriage now? *(Perhaps, now that David is himself married to someone who turned out to be less than he hoped, Aunt Betsey feels he has the ability to understand.)*

16. To what does David attribute the fact that all of the servants he employs seem to "go bad"? *(He says they are given too many opportunities to get away with things, and that it is unfair to them.)*

17. What are the consequences of David's attempts to "form Dora's mind"? *(Her mind seems to already be formed and quite unlikely to change. She says it best: "It's better for me to be stupid than uncomfortable, isn't it?")*

18. When does Dora's health begin to weaken? *(after she loses a baby)* What do you think is foreshadowed in the last few sentences of Chapter 48? How might the Jip/Dora parallel be involved?

19. What comes of Traddles and David's meeting with Mr. Micawber? *(Micawber reveals that Uriah Heep is guilty of terrible treachery, and that he, Micawber, plans to expose Heep.)*

20. **Prediction:** What do you think Micawber will have to say about Heep?

Writing Idea

At the Strongs, David heard two phrases:

> "There can be no disparity in marriage like unsuitably of mind and purpose."
>
> "...the first mistaken impulse of an undisciplined heart."

Why do these phrases keep recurring to David? How are they related to his life now?

Chapters L-LV

Vocabulary

repine 660	expeditiously 661	carrion 666	athwart 670
reproach 675	dexterity 680	impostor 686	benignant 687
dissipated 691	knavish 692	impetuosity 693	consummate 694
deponents 698	inanition 701	augur 714	defalcation 719
impertinence 723	dissuade 729	singular 737	insensible 737

Discussion Questions

1. What do you know immediately from the title of Chapter 50, "Mr. Peggotty's Dream Comes True"? *(that Emily has been found)*

2. After Martha comes for David, there are seven paragraphs before we get to Emily, and two are quite long and descriptive. Why do you suppose they were included? *(to build suspense)*

3. Did Emily do a very good job of defending herself against Rosa Dartle? *(no; She is apologetic, self-effacing.)* Do you think David should have intervened?

4. How would Emily's situation be viewed by society today? Martha's situation? *(Answers will vary.)*

5. What did Emily do after she escaped from Littimer? *(She was taken in by a woman who lived near the beach who arranged for her to go to France. There Emily worked at an inn, but left when she spotted "that snake" and came to England. Afraid her uncle had not forgiven her, she went to London, where a woman Emily thought to be a friend led her very nearly into prostitution. Just in time, she was saved by Martha.)*

6. Where does Mr. Peggotty plan to take Emily to start a new life? *(Australia)* What will become of Mrs. Gummidge, Peggotty, and Ham? *(Mr. Peggotty plans to leave Mrs. Gummidge behind, but give her an allowance; Peggotty will remain in Yarmouth, and look after Ham, who needs someone to talk to.)*

7. What two things does Mr. Peggotty need to do before he leaves for Australia? *(return to the Steerforths the money Emily sent in her letters; tell Ham she has been found)*

8. How has Martha been given a new lease on life by being instrumental in returning Emily to her uncle? *(She can now have some self-respect; Mr. Omer mentions that he never thought she was all bad, wants to help her out.)*

9. When David visits Ham, how does Ham prove true to his character? *(He blames himself for pushing his affections on Emily, wants her to forgive him and to bear no guilt about him. He also asks David to make sure Mr. Peggotty knows how much Ham cares about him, and how grateful he is for having had him as a surrogate father.)*

10. Why is Mrs. Gummidge happy at the end of Chapter 51? *(She has convinced Mr. Peggotty to let her go along to Australia.)*

11. Who goes down to Canterbury for the meeting with Micawber and Heep? *(Traddles, David, Aunt Betsey, Mr. Dick)*

12. Why, on page 686, is David troubled by the sound of the bells? *(They make him think of Dora and of those who die young. He is worried about her.)*

13. Why have Traddles and Mr. Micawber been in communication? *(Traddles has been advising Mr. Micawber on the legal aspects of what he is about to do.)*

14. What is ironic about Aunt Betsey's remark to Uriah, "I think you are pretty constant to the promise of your youth"? *(What sounds like a compliment is actually an insult—she spotted him for a scoundrel the first time she met him.)*

15. How does Uriah's true character show itself during the meeting? *(First he calls Micawber a dissipated fellow and orders him out; then he begins accusing the group of forming a conspiracy, reminds David he was once the scum of society, threatens Aunt Betsey with revealing knowledge about her husband, and Agnes with her father's ruin.)*

16. What legal instrument does Traddles produce? *(Mr. Wickfield's power of attorney)*

17. What information does Micawber reveal? *(He often had borrowed money from Heep, and in exchange had to assist in the falsification of records and in keeping Mr. Wickfield totally in the dark about what was happening. Heep obtained Mr. Wickfield's signature on important documents by telling him they were unimportant, filtered off money he pretended was needed for business expenses, forged Mr. Wickfield's name, convinced Mr. Wickfield the firm was bankrupt, etc.)*

18. Why has Aunt Betsey not said anything about the loss of her fortune until now? *(She thought it had been lost or stolen by Mr. Wickfield; now she realizes the loss was fabricated by Heep, and she demands its return.)*

19. What proof is offered of Heep's dishonesties? *(An account book he kept; he threw it in the fire, but Micawber saved it while the figures were still legible.)*

20. What does Traddles demand of Heep? *(He must hand over the deed of relinquishment given to him by Mr. Wickfield; he must make restitution to all who have been wronged.)*

21. Mr. Micawber's speech as he is reunited with his family is quite melodramatic as he contemplates what will happen to them now. What does Aunt Betsey suggest? *(emigration to Australia; Now that her money will be returned to her, she is more than willing to give him a loan.)*

22. Why is Aunt Betsey sorry that Jip no longer growls at her? *(Like his mistress, Jip is growing feeble, and his behavior reminds her of Dora's condition.)*

23. Why is Dora happy that she is dying? *(She fears that if she lived David would have grown very bored with her, and that she would never have been able to improve.)* Does this make any sense, or is she just being foolish as usual?

24. How is the Jip/Dora parallel carried out in Chapter 53? *(Both die at the same time.)*

25. Agnes suggests that David go abroad to relieve his depression about Dora's death. Before he leaves, he decides to do what? *(wait until the emigrants leave, and wait until matters are settled with Heep)*

26. What will Agnes do now that the law firm is liquidated? *(She will open a school and take care of her father.)*

27. Traddles points out a reason that Micawber should be particularly congratulated. What is it? *(He could have blackmailed Heep for his silence and probably done quite well financially.)*

28. Why do the police come looking for Micawber? *(Heep has turned his IOUs from Micawber over to the police, hoping to have Micawber imprisoned for debt.)* What is the result? *(Aunt Betsey pays his IOUs and keeps him out of prison.)*

29. Where has Aunt Betsey been spending her time, and why is she so quiet? *(Her husband died in the hospital; she was going to visit him. He was, at the end, very sorry for all the trouble he caused her.)*

30. Why does David go to Yarmouth? *(to give Ham the letter Emily wrote to him)* What happens on his way? *(There is a terrible storm.)* What happens when he arrives in Yarmouth? *(He sees a ship offshore, about to break up and sink, and a man swims out to try to rescue a survivor who is clinging to the mast. The rescuer is Ham; the survivor is Steerforth. Both men die.)* Do you find this train of events believable, or is it overly melodramatic and too coincidental?

31. **Prediction:** How will Mrs. Steerforth and Rosa Dartle react to the news of Steerforth's death? How will Mr. Peggotty and Emily react when they learn that Ham died trying to save the man who ruined their lives and Ham's?

Writing Idea

After the emigrants leave and the Heep affair is settled, David will be going abroad for a period of about three years. If you suffered a traumatic event in your life and could go anywhere you wanted for three years to think things over, where would it be? Why?

Chapters LVI-LXIV

Vocabulary

emigrants 744	desolate 754	despondency 754	sustaining 755
perplexities 759	aggregate 759	obscurity 761	indomitable 762
decamped 764	negus 772	perdition 774	loquacious 774
magistrate 786	repasts 788	admonitions 789	neophytes 790
indignant 792	discomfiture 801	robust 803	patriarch 814

Discussion Questions

1. Why does David go to see Mrs. Steerforth? *(He feels it's his responsibility to tell her about her son's death.)* What is her reaction to the news? *(She doesn't seem to understand, and is in shock.)* Is Rosa Dartle supportive? *(Not at first; she attacks Mrs. Steerforth, accusing her of making her son into a monster, and saying that she always loved him better. Finally, Rosa collapses into tears and tries to comfort Mrs. Steerforth.)*

2. David might have reacted angrily to Steerforth's death, blaming him for Ham's death. What do you suppose Dickens was saying about David's character? *(David has worshipped Steerforth from the beginning, and his feelings for him have never really changed. He will always "think of him at his best.")*

3. Do you think David was right to withhold the news of Ham's death from Mr. Peggotty and Emily? Why or why not? What might the consequences have been if he had told them?

4. As the Micawbers prepare for their journey to Australia, how do they change? *(They are all clothed as if they are going off to the wilds, and Mr. Micawber looks quite at home in his new oilcloth suit and straw hat.)*

5. What happens to Micawber as he is making the punch for the farewell toast? *(He is arrested because of Heep turning him in again for debt.)* How is the problem solved? *(David pays the money to get him out of jail.)*

6. The Micawbers' mode of dress has changed—but what about them has stayed the same? *(As usual, they are filled with hope and confidence about the new venture.)* As you read Chapter 57, did you imagine they would do well in Australia?

7. What surprise traveler does David meet at the boat? *(Martha)* What does this tell you about Mr. Peggotty's character? *(He is no user of people, and would always repay a debt tenfold if he possibly could.)*

8. As David wanders around Europe, what losses does he feel and grieve? *(Dora, Steerforth, Emily, and his own feelings of safety and love when he was very young and lived at Blunderstone.)*

9. The healing power of Nature is a frequent theme in literature. How is this idea brought out in Chapter 58? *(After months of despondency, David comes into a beautiful valley in the Swiss Alps. There he is finally able to weep for all he has lost.)*

10. A character who has been in the novel almost all along also has healing powers for David. Who is it, and how does she help? *(Agnes writes to David regularly, offering him support and encouragement.)*

11. What are some activities that restore David and bring him out of his despondency? *(He resumes writing, makes many friends in the little Swiss village, exercises regularly, and learns about the countries he visits.)*

12. How do David's feelings about Agnes change while he is in Europe? *(He begins to realize she was the one he relied on all along, that she would make a wonderful wife.)*

13. How long does David stay away from England? *(three years)* Upon his return, who does he visit first, and what is the situation there? *(He goes to see Traddles, who is now married and surrounded by Sophy's five adoring sisters in a small apartment.)*

14. Dickens was often critical of the wealthy. How does Traddles prove that "money can't buy happiness"? *(Although not well-off materially, Traddles is exceedingly happy, and so are those around him. His life is filled with warmth and love, and that is all that seems to matter.)*

15. Why is Mr. Chillip included in Chapter 59? *(Chillip provides the information that the Murdstones have treated Murdstone's new wife the same way they treated David's mother. Chillip gives confirmation to David's belief that the evil Murdstones will pay for their greed and dishonesty someday.)*

16. Did Janet continue to take Aunt Betsey's advice to her to renounce mankind? *(No. She married the tavern keeper.)*

17. What is Mr. Dick doing? *(happily copying everything he can find)*

18. Why do you think Aunt Betsey tells David that Agnes "has an attachment"? *(Answers will vary.)*

19. Why is it so difficult for David to tell Agnes how he really feels about her? *(He doesn't want to jeopardize the brother-sister relationship by trying to change it to something she may not want.)* Have you ever been in a similar situation?

20. What explanation does Mr. Wickfield give for his wife's death? *(She had married him against her father's wishes, and his rejection of the marriage broke her heart.)* Is it really possible to die of a broken heart, do you think?

21. Why does Creakle contact Traddles? *(to show him the "perfect prison system")* Who are the "two interesting penitents" in Chapter 61? *(Heep and Littimer)* What are the components of the "perfect system"? *(solitary confinement, good food, religious zeal)* Does it seem to be working for the two prisoners? *(No. Dickens pokes fun at the prison system here and shows Littimer and Heep to be even more repulsive than they were before due to their sanctimonious attitudes and their warnings to repent. David and Traddles see that they have simply become more hypocritical than ever.)*

22. How did Littimer happen to get caught? *(Miss Mowcher tripped him and hung on to him like a bulldog until the authorities came for him.)*

© Novel Units, Inc.

37

23. What does Agnes tell David that changes his life from that point on? *("I have loved you all my life.")* What last wish of Dora's makes the union even more poignant? *(Dora hoped that only Agnes would replace her as David's wife.)*

24. Events in Chapter 63 and 64 take place ten years after the last chapter. Why do you think Dickens included them? *(to let the reader know the following: David and Agnes' marriage is happy and blessed with children; the Peggottys, Micawbers, and friends—including Mr. Mell—are doing well in Australia; Peggotty is now taking care of Aunt Betsey, who is old but still quite feisty; Doctor Strong still works on his dictionary; Julia Mills has married a wealthy Scotchman and been ruined by money; Traddles is destined to be a judge; Mrs. Steerforth was driven crazy by the loss of her son.)*

25. A more modern novel would probably end with Chapter 62, and let the reader supply from his or her own imagination what happened in the coming years. Which kind of ending do you prefer, and why? *(Answers will vary.)*

Post-reading Discussion Questions

1. Make a list of the "good guys" and "bad guys" in this novel. Where possible, jot down what became of them. For the most part, do goodness and justice prevail? Do characters end up getting what they deserve? Do you think real life works out like that?

2. Consider the character of Agnes. Is she believable, or too perfect to be realistic? Does she ever do anything wrong, or show any poor judgement? *(Agnes is the Victorian "ideal heroine." If Dickens was writing today, critics would probably find her too idealized, but since she appears in a Victorian novel, she fulfills her role well. Students may mention that she should have done something about Heep taking over her father's business, but it would be unusual for a Victorian gentlewoman to meddle in business affairs.)*

3. Mrs. Markleham and Mrs. Steerforth are both forceful characters. What traits do they have in common? *(Both are controlling and materialistic.)*

4. Edward Murdstone, Mr. Creakle, Mr. Spenlow, Steerforth, Uriah Heep, and Littimer are all evil-doers in the novel, but they represent different kinds of evil. Use the diagram below to organize your thoughts about their character flaws. (The chart has been started.) Then use the completed chart to write an essay comparing the characters.

Character	selfish	comical	materialistic	haughty	scheming	sadistic	spoiled
Mr. Creakle		X				X	
Littimer							
Murdstone							
Mr. Spenlow							
Steerforth							
Uriah Heep							

5. This novel begins, "Whether I shall turn out to be the hero of my own life...these pages must show." What do the pages show? Is David the "hero of his own life"? Explain your answer. *(Throughout the novel, David is being tested by life. Examples: the tyranny of Creakle, survival as a ten-year old alone in London, disappointment in his marriage to Dora, his aunt's bankruptcy, his wife's death, the tragic Steerforth-Emily affair. He not only meets these challenges with strength and a steadily growing maturity, he remains compassionate, kind, and strong.)*

6. How does David gain control over his "undisciplined heart"? *(As he matures and suffers through numerous tribulations, David realizes it is the slow, steady fire of Agnes that has kept him alive and determined to do the right thing. His love for her is a combination of emotion and rational thinking, as opposed to the impulsive blindness of his love for Dora.)*

7. David is a strong character, yet is quite tender-hearted as well. How does this "family resemblance" show itself in his Aunt Betsey? *(When Aunt Betsey appears at David's birth, she seems quite forceful. Later, we see her gentle side as she takes in Mr. Dick and David, accepts Peggotty, loans money to the Micawbers, and intuitively knows that Agnes and David belong together.)*

8. Dickens' use of coincidence is sometimes called a weakness of this and other novels of his. Actually, coincidence was acceptable and even expected by Victorian readers. Choose several of the coincidental events in the novel and either defend or criticize Dickens for using them.

9. What types of conflict do you find in *David Copperfield?* *(inner conflict in several characters [David, Emily, Steerforth], conflict with society [Mr. Micawber, Martha, Emily, the pomposity of the wealthy, the courts, the prison system], character vs. character [David and others conflict with the Murdstones, Creakle, Heep, Littimer ,the Steerforths, Rosa Dartle, etc.], conflict with nature [the storm at sea that kills Ham and Steerforth])*

10. There are several themes in *David Copperfield.* Looking at types of conflict is often a key to theme. In group discussion, consider the main conflicts and their resolutions; then arrive at a mutually-agreed-upon list of themes you feel Dickens had in mind as he wrote the novel. *(Some possible answers: the passage from youth to maturity; the nature of true love; good vs. evil—with good winning; the basic goodness of simple people vs. the haughty materialism and artificiality of the wealthy; the bureaucratic waste in government; the tragedy of child labor; love conquers all.)*

11. Creakle definitely believed in—and in fact enjoyed administering—corporal punishment at Salem House School. Use a plan like the one on the following page to research this question as it applies to schools today. Present your findings in one of the following forms: a position paper for a news magazine, a television documentary, a panel discussion or talk show, or a detailed letter to your principal.

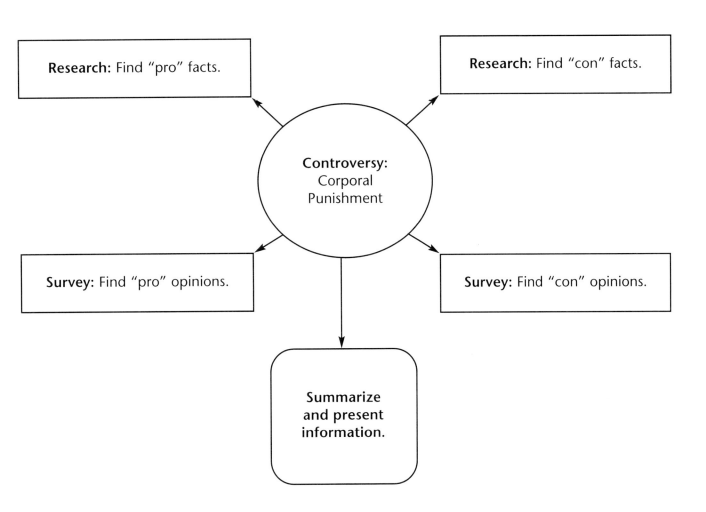

Research: Find "pro" facts.

Research: Find "con" facts.

Controversy:
Corporal
Punishment

Survey: Find "pro" opinions.

Survey: Find "con" opinions.

Summarize
and present
information.

Post-reading Extension Activities

Melodrama
Melodrama is the use of highly sensational or emotional actions and language to provoke an emotional response in the viewer or reader.

There are a number of melodramatic scenes in this novel. With a partner or small group, present one of the following (or a scene of your own choosing) in drama form. When you are practicing, decide which non-dialogue sections the narrator should read, and which sections should be shown to the audience through facial expression, physical action, etc.

(a)   a young and terrified David trying to recite his lessons at Blunderstone
(b)   Steerforth's denunciation of Mr. Mell
(c)   Rosa Dartle's encounter with Emily after her return from Europe
(d)   Rosa Dartle's castigation of Mrs. Steerforth when they learn of James' death
(e)   the night of Dora's death
(f)   Micawber's exposure of Uriah Heep

Art
1.   Choose one of the evil characters in the novel, and one of the good characters. Draw a picture in which the two characters are in conflict in a symbolic representation of good versus evil.

2.   Design and write a postcard Emily sends to David from Australia.

Famous Quotations
Make a list of quotes typical of various characters (i.e., Micawber: "Something will turn up!" Barkis: "Barkis is willin'.") Write each quote on a small piece of paper and put them in a hat or box. In small groups, a leader should draw out one quote at a time and read it to the group. The student who identifies the speaker is given the slip of paper. The student with the most quotes wins.

Culinary
The English have always had tea late in the afternoon. Find out more about this custom. In addition to tea, what would be served? Write an article that might appear in a magazine about cooking. Include the history and explanation of the custom as well as several recipes for foods that are served.

Time Line
Beginning with David's birth and ending with the birth of his youngest child, make a time line showing the important events in his life.

Creative Writing
1.   The wedding of Agnes and David is not described. Imagine they wrote their own vows for the ceremony, and write each set of vows. Present them to your class in a mock wedding ceremony.

2. Imagine you are David, applying for the job with the newspaper as a Parliamentary reporter. Write a letter to the newspaper's editor explaining why you believe you deserve the job.

3. According to Shakespeare, "The course of true love never did run smooth." Do you think this is always true? Write a short replacement for Chapter 64 that changes the story and proves Shakespeare's maxim—at least in the case of David and Agnes.

4. If Dickens was around today, he might be a syndicated newspaper columnist who wrote socially-critical columns about the government. Write the sort of column you believe Dickens would have submitted on a current political issue. Remember, Dickens rarely lost his sense of humor, particularly where the government was concerned. (Check your newspaper for some examples before you begin writing.)

5. Many of the names of Dickens' classic characters live on in everyday conversation. For instance, you might say about someone you know, "She's a real dumb Dora" or "He's a regular Micawber." Think of some of the other characters in the novel. Do you know anyone who is as creepy as Uriah Heep, as pompous as Mr. Spenlow, or as good-natured and happy as Tommy Traddles? Write a brief sketch comparing the person you know with the Dickens character.

6. Write the newspaper article appearing in *The Yarmouth Tattler* the day after Ham and Steerforth die in the storm. (*The Tattler* happens to be a gossipy, sensationalistic newspaper. To make sure of your article being accepted for publication, you will have to include some gossip about the characters involved.)

7. Many of Mr. Micawber's letters appear in the novel. Write David's reply to the last letter from Micawber, at the end of Chapter 63.

8. Write an elegy (mourning poem) about Dora. For an example, read Gray's "Elegy in a Country Churchyard."

9. Write the dialogue for a conversation Agnes and David have about Emily and Steerforth shortly after Mr. Peggotty's visit from Australia.

10. An epic poem is a long narrative poem that tells about the trials and triumphs of a hero. Write a poem in epic style about David's life. For some examples, see *Beowulf*, *The Iliad*, and *The Odyssey*. Whitman's *Leaves of Grass*, sometimes called an American epic, may be an easier example to follow.

Notes